MEN FROM THE VILLAGE DEEP IN THE MOUNTAINS

DEEP IN THE MOUNTAINS

And Other Japanese Folk Tales

MEN FROM THE VILLAGE DEEP IN THE MOUNTAINS

And Other Japanese Folk Tales

Translated and Illustrated by
GARRETT BANG

MACMILLAN PUBLISHING CO., INC.
New York
COLLIER MACMILLAN PUBLISHERS
London

Macmillan Publishing Co., Inc., 866 Third Avenue
New York, N.Y. 10022
Collier-Macmillan Canada Ltd., Toronto, Ontario
Library of Congress catalog card number: 72–92431
Printed in the United States of America

1 2 3 4 5 6 7 8 9 10

ACKNOWLEDGMENTS

"The Crusty Old Badger" and "The Strange Folding Screen" are
translated by kind permission of Japan UNI Agency, Inc., from stories
in *Nihon No Minwa*, edited by Minoru Kakiuchi, published by
Miraisha Publishers.

All other stories are translated by kind permission of Iwanami Shoten,
Publishers, from *Nihon No Mukashibanashi*, edited by Keigo Seki,
published by Iwanami Shoten, Publishers, Tokyo, 1956.
Copyright © 1956 by Keigo Seki.

Library of Congress Cataloging in Publication Data

Bang, Garrett, comp.
  Men from the village deep in the mountains and other Japanese folk
tales.

  CONTENTS: Men from the village deep in the mountains.
—Patches.—The stone statue and the grass hat. [etc.]
  1. Tales, Japanese. [1. Folklore—Japan]
I. Title.
PZ8.1.B227Me   398.2'0952   72–92431   ISBN 0–02–708350–0

For Seiichi and Masako Matsumoto

Contents

MEN FROM THE VILLAGE DEEP IN THE MOUNTAINS

DEEP IN THE MOUNTAINS

And Other Japanese Folk Tales

Men from the Village Deep in the Mountains

In a village deep in the mountains there once lived three men, Crafty Yasohachi, Stingy Kichiyomu and Dull-witted Hikoichi. It isn't known how long ago they lived, or even whether they all lived at one time, but stories of the three trickled down from the mountains to the towns. The townspeople would sit around a table covered with a quilt, their feet toasting on a grill over a hole in which red coals were kept burning. They would sit there, eating oranges, drinking tea and telling stories until far into the night.

Crafty Yasohachi Climbs to Heaven

It was early spring, and the field under Yasohachi's care was full of hard clumps of dirt that needed to be smoothed and plowed before the rice could be planted. But Yasohachi had other things to do.

The days went by and the field remained unplowed, still Yasohachi had other matters to attend to. One of these was to put up a sign in the village, which read:

"On Sunday at the Hour of the Monkey, Yasohachi will climb from his field to heaven."

The master heard about this and came to Yasohachi's house.

"You worthless man!" he cried. "Your field lies bumpy as the back of a toad, and you spend your time doing magic tricks!"

Yasohachi smiled his toothy smile and motioned toward the door.

"Come with me now, if it pleases you, sir," he said. "It's just about time for the climb."

The two men walked out of the door and over to the unplowed field, where a crowd of villagers were standing around a pole stuck upright in the ground.

Yasohachi marched up to the pole and grabbed it tightly, then with a flourish of his free hand he turned to the crowd.

"Most honorable spectators!" he announced. "You are about to see a spectacle such as you will never witness again in all your lives!"

He took hold of the pole with both hands and lifted himself up. He reached up and hoisted himself higher. The pole began to lean. The villagers gasped and scurried out of the way as the pole and Yasohachi came crashing to the ground.

Yasohachi stood up. Calm, unfluttered, he brushed himself off and picked up the pole. Several paces away he again stuck it into the ground, deeper than before, so that it was as sturdy as a sapling. He grabbed it with both hands and again hoisted himself up. Twice he reached and twice he pulled; he was halfway up the pole! He reached up again. The pole swayed, the villagers ran out of the way, and Yasohachi and the pole toppled over.

This continued time after time, until finally the villagers got disgusted and went home, muttering.

"I never believed he could do it anyway."

"The idea! Climbing to heaven on a bamboo pole!"

Yasohachi and the master were left alone. The master scowled and pulled his ear, looking at Yasohachi. Crafty Yasohachi smiled and pointed to the field where they stood. There was not a single clod of hard dirt in sight; the trampling crowd had smoothed it flat as the morning sea!

Stingy Kichiyomu and the Rice Thieves

Stingy Kichiyomu was a miser. He was so stingy that he ate no rice at all for lunch, but sat sucking a toothpick instead.

One day he was sitting on his cushion in a spot of sun on the porch, when a servant from the master's house came running up with a package wrapped in bamboo leaves.

"Two fresh sea bream!" the servant said, bowing. "The master was given a basket of fish by a relative who lives by the sea. He sends these down to you as a gift."

Kichiyomu's wife took the package carefully into her hands. She folded back the leaves and looked. Two fresh fish, red and fat! She bowed again and again to the servant.

Fresh fish! They were lucky to have fish even on holidays, and then it was usually dried and salted. Two fresh sea bream!

She ran inside to cut them up and boil the rice for dinner.

Stingy Kichiyomu stood up and left his cushion in the spot of sun. He stalked inside and followed his wife all the way into the kitchen. He watched her for a moment, then suddenly snatched the fish away and marched back outside with them.

His wife turned and ran after him, pulling at his arm. Stingy Kichiyomu stomped over to the edge of the porch and, in a fury, threw the fish into the field.

"Rice thieves!" he yelled after them.

"What are you doing?" his wife cried. "What are you doing?"

"Hah!" her husband answered, glaring at the two dead fish. "When we eat fish as good as these two, we always eat twice as much rice as usual to go with them. It's the same as if the fish stole the extra rice themselves. Rice thieves!"

And Stingy Kichiyomu went back to sit on his cushion in the spot of sun.

Dull-Witted Hikoichi, the Mortar and the Worn-Out Horse

Hikoichi was strong, fat and dull-witted. One day the master asked him to go fetch a heavy stone mortar from a neighboring village. As the mortar was too much for a man to handle, the master gave Hikoichi a horse to carry it back.

"The old nag isn't strong," the master said. "You're welcome to ride it to the village if you like, but you'd better walk along beside it once it has the mortar on its back."

Hikoichi folded his hands across his fat belly, looked at the horse and nodded in agreement. The poor animal was so worn out it could hardly walk, even with nothing on its back but its own hide. Its ribs stuck out so far a man could stick his finger deep between them, and still not touch its pelt. Hikoichi mounted, and rode slowly off down the road.

What was his master's surprise that evening, when he saw the old horse stumbling back into the yard, wheezing and gasping, almost dead. Hikoichi sat proudly in the saddle holding the mortar; the horse was carrying him and the stone mortar as well!

"Hikoichi! Hikoichi!" cried the master. "You did exactly what I asked you not to do. You've nearly killed the horse with all that weight!"

"But, master," Hikoichi replied in dismay, "you told me not to ride it once it was carrying the mortar. Well, the horse was much too weak for that, so I decided to carry the mortar myself and then the horse would only have to carry me."

Crafty Yasohachi and the Flea Medicine

One summer Yasohachi had to take a trip. There was only one inn a day's walk from the village and luckily he reached it just after dark. He was hot and tired and covered with dust, and as soon as he had finished his bath he fell straight into bed.

Fleas! The bed was full of them! There were so many fleas he couldn't sleep a wink, and tossed and turned and scratched himself all night. By morning he was covered with itchy red bites.

Since there was no other inn close by, Yasohachi knew he would have to stop there again on his way home. He thought with dread of another flea-bitten night.

7

Just as he was about to leave, Crafty Yasohachi turned to the innkeeper:

"Sir," he said, with great hesitation, "I hope you don't mind my mentioning this, as I'm sure you already know it, but. . . ."

"What is it?" the innkeeper asked suspiciously.

"Uuuuuuhto," said Yasohachi. "Did you know that the medicine shop in Sagawa is giving an even better price for fleas than it did before? It seems the medicine they make from them has excellent results."

"Medicine from fleas?" the innkeeper asked in amazement. "I never heard of that!"

"Uuuuuuhto," said Crafty Yasohachi, looking thoughtful. "I'll be coming back this way in a few days, and if you like I'll take any fleas you have to Sagawa with me."

The innkeeper was so delighted he followed Yasohachi all the way out to the gate.

Several days later, Yasohachi finished his business and stopped at the inn on his way home. This time he enjoyed a long, undisturbed sleep.

Next morning, he was getting ready to leave, when the innkeeper rushed up to him. He held a basket covered with a cloth in his hands.

"Yasohachi, sir!" he cried. "I have the fleas for you! Aren't you going to sell them for me as you promised?" He held out the basket and lifted the edge of the cloth which covered it.

Yasohachi bent to look inside the basket. Ah! There were hundreds, thousands, even millions of tiny black fleas in it. Yasohachi quickly set the cloth back over the fleas and straightened up. With an embarrassed gesture, he turned to the innkeeper.

"I'm awfully sorry," he said, "but there's one thing I forgot to tell you. The medicine shop only takes them if they're strung on wire skewers, twenty-four to a wire. If you can have that done by the next time I come, I'll be happy to take them in for you."

Yasohachi bowed courteously and walked away, as the innkeeper stood staring after him.

Dull-Witted Hikoichi and the Duck Soup

Hikoichi was once invited to the master's house for supper.

"I've just shot a duck!" the master told him happily. "We're going to have a whole pot of duck soup!"

Duck soup! Duck soup was one thing Hikoichi had heard about all of his life, but had never once tasted, or even smelled. He thought with pleasure of the evening ahead.

The day of the supper he walked up the hill to the master's house. The table was set. He sat down and slowly, politely, lifted the lid from his bowl.

What? It looked like a soup made of radishes! He sniffed it. It smelled like radish soup. He picked up the bowl and cautiously drank a few mouthfuls. It was radish soup, exactly the same as the soup they had had at home the night before. When he looked closely, he thought he saw a few strings of some dark meat in the broth, but he couldn't be sure. He swallowed the rest of the soup, thanked the master for dinner and walked home.

Several days later, he was talking with the master when the subject of ducks came up.

"You say you really shoot these ducks with guns?" Dull-witted Hikoichi asked in disbelief.

"Why, of course," the master replied.

"Do these ducks have green heads which they sway back and forth?" asked Hikoichi.

"Well, they do sway their heads about sometimes,"

the master answered. "And some do have green heads, though they are quite rare and I've never shot one myself. What a pleasure it would be to shoot a real green-head!"

"Oh, good," cried Hikoichi. "I know of a place where you can shoot as many green-heads as you like, just on the far side of my house."

"What? Why didn't you tell me before?" cried the master. "I'll come tomorrow evening."

He started to walk off, then turned back to Hikoichi.

"Don't worry about supper," he said. "I'll bring a bite of something for us to eat."

The master arrived, late the next afternoon. In one hand he held a shiny gun, in the other a lacquered picnic box. Hikoichi led the way to the field beyond his house, and the two men sat down and waited in silence.

They sat for a while, but there was no sign of a duck. The master opened the picnic box.

What a feast! There were rice balls filled with mushrooms and beancurd and eggs, wrapped in delicate seaweed. There were dried fish and smoked fish and pickles soaked in the lees of wine. There were many salads: cucumber and shrimp, spinach and sesame seeds, even lotus root and thin-sliced water chestnuts.

Hikoichi quietly ate his fill. The master only picked at the food. He held his gun ready and kept a close watch on the fields.

The sun went down; the fields were almost dark. There hadn't been the quack of a duck all evening.

Hikoichi turned to the master. "Well, sir," he asked: "How do you like the green-heads? Aren't they a splendid sight?"

The master stared hard into the dusk. There wasn't a duck to be seen.

"Where do you see any?" he asked eagerly.

"Why, sir," replied Hikoichi, pointing, "the field is full of them!"

The master looked. The field was full of healthy green radish tops, waving in the evening breeze!

Stingy Kichiyomu and the Iron Hammer

One day Kichiyomu was sitting on his cushion on the porch, when he called to his wife to come out for a moment.

He pointed to the boards of the porch.

"The nails are sticking out there," he said. "Go see if you can borrow an iron hammer from the neighbors so that I can hammer them back in."

His wife went out, but soon returned empty-handed.

"I asked them for a hammer to hammer in the nails," she said. "They asked me if the nails were of bamboo, of wood or of iron. When I told them they were iron nails, they said the iron nails would wear down the iron hammer, and refused to lend it to us."

Kichiyomu jumped up in a rage.

"Stingy misers!" he shouted, storming into the house. "There's nothing to do now but use that iron hammer of our own!"

Patches

There was once an actor named Patches who worked with a group of traveling players. One day, while on the road, he received a letter saying that his father was very sick.

Patches was worried, and left for home at once, taking along only his bag of disguises. He walked all day, and by night he had only one more mountain to cross before he reached home. A teahouse stood at the foot of the mountain, and he decided to stop for something to eat.

An old woman served him hot tea, but shook her head gravely when she heard that he was going to cross the mountain that night.

"Don't cross the mountain after dark," she said, "for there is a serpent up there who comes out at night and swallows whomever he finds."

She told him of other travelers who had left her teashop at nightfall, heedless of her warning, and who were never seen again.

But Patches wanted to hurry home to his father; he left the teashop and set off to climb the dark mountain. It was just past midnight when he reached the top, where a small shrine stood in the shadows of the moon.

"That's a good place to rest," thought Patches, and he went inside and lay down. But he had no sooner touched the ground when a tall white-haired old man appeared in the doorway.

"Who are you?" the old man asked, and his voice was silky smooth.

"I'm Patches," the actor replied.

But the old man misunderstood him and thought he had said, "I'm Badger."

"Oh," the man said eagerly. "I've heard badgers can change themselves into all sorts of things. Show me some other creature you can change into."

Patches opened his mouth to tell the stranger he was mistaken, but the old man interrupted him.

"Well, now," he said, grinning, "I'd like to see just how good you are, to find out if you're better than I

16

am. I'm not really an old man at all; I'm the serpent of the mountain."

Patches closed his mouth. He gritted his teeth together to keep them from chattering, and opened his bag of disguises.

Quickly he pulled out a lady's wig, then painted his mouth with red lipstick and covered his face with a white paste and powder. He swayed and simpered like a dancing girl, and the old man clapped his hands in delight. "You're better than I'd ever imagined," he cried.

The two of them talked about this and that, and after a long while the old serpent-man asked Patches, "What do you hate most in the world?"

"Money," said Patches. "What about you?"

"Ugh," the old man said. "I hate stale tobacco tar and the juice from sour persimmons. If one or the other touches my body, I cannot move a scale, and I'm forced to lie powerless for hours. If the humans knew, it would be the end of me. You and I are beasts of the wild and have to help one another. I can tell you this with trust. But people must never know."

Soon after the old man bowed to Patches and disappeared.

Patches immediately leaped out of the shrine and ran down the mountain as fast as he could go, until at last he reached his own village. Day was dawning, and he met two woodcutters on their way to work. Patches told them about his meeting with the serpent-man, and how the creature could be chased away. He then went to his own house to care for his father, but the woodcutters, instead of going to work, returned to the village.

They knocked on the door of each house and told the villagers to save their old tobacco tar and their sticky sour persimmon juice. Before long they had collected a great deal of each, and smeared the foul stuff on the trees of the mountain forest. And the serpent was forced to flee to higher, lonelier mountains.

But the serpent knew that it was Patches who had given away his secret, and before he left he resolved to take revenge. He found out where Patches lived. Stealthily he slithered to the gate of the house, and onto the door. When he found the door was locked, he crawled up the wall, and over the roof to the smoke hole. He coiled himself around it and peered inside. Patches was sitting at his father's bedside. The serpent slowly opened the smoke hole and slid his head inside.

"This is my revenge!" he cried.

And into the house he dropped a huge pile of gold and silver coins. Then he fled away into the high and lonely mountains.

The Stone Statue and the Grass Hat

Long ago there lived a couple who were so poor that they had nothing with which to celebrate on New Year's Eve. The woman turned to her husband and said:

"Why don't we sell our empty silk spools? That might give us enough money to buy some red beans and rice."

Her husband agreed, and set off for town with the empty spools. "Spools, spools! Empty silk spools!" Back and forth he went, from one end of town to the other, chilled to the bone and his voice hoarse with yelling. But on this day before New Year's in this particular town, not a soul wanted so much as to look at used-up silk spools.

Still, back and forth he plied his poor wares, until the sun went down and lights appeared in the houses and shops. There was nothing for him to do but return home as he had come.

As he was leaving the shopping district, he saw an old man coming from the opposite direction, selling a grass hat.

"Spools! Spools! Empty spools!"

"A grass hat! A grass hat! Who wants to buy a grass hat?"

The two men looked at each other as they met. The old hat-seller stopped.

"I've been trying to sell my hat all day," he said, "and my throat is sore from shouting."

The other thought of all the things he would have liked to buy. "I guess nobody wants either a grass hat or empty spools on New Year's Eve," he said. "We should be selling rice or fish." And he laughed to think of what they had been trying to do.

The old man looked at him.

22

"It's not a laughing matter," he said. "I can't go back home with the same goods I took with me. Listen," he went on. "You probably don't want to take your spools back either. Why don't we exchange them? At least we'll each have something different."

And so the man exchanged his empty spools for a grass hat. Out of the town he trudged and onto the road leading home. Just as he was crossing a wide flat meadow, flakes of snow began to fall, and before long they had turned into a heavy blizzard.

The man put one foot in front of the other and walked on blindly, until suddenly he bumped into something cold and hard. He looked up; it was a stone statue of Jizo, the guardian of children and travelers. Naked as a babe the statue stood, right in the middle of the storm.

"Oh, dear," the man mumbled to himself. "Jizo-sama must be dreadfully cold, out in this snowstorm and without a stitch of clothing on."

He took out the hat he had received for the spools, and put it on the statue's head. Then slowly, sadly and empty-handed, he plodded home.

His wife had expected him to come back with rice and red beans, and was waiting, ready with a pot of boiling water. He came in from the dark and shook the snow from his clothes. Then he told her what had happened. She only smiled and comforted him.

"Oh, good," she said. "We couldn't have used the grass hat tonight anyway, and it was the best thing you could have done to give it to Jizo-sama."

Then, since there was nothing to eat, they went to bed.

Just as the sky was getting light, the husband and wife awoke with a start. The blizzard was still raging, and clumps of snow thumped against the house. But with the thumping of the snow there was another sound.

"Krunch, grunch," they heard. "Krunch, grunch. Krunch, grunch."

The husband and wife sat up in bed. "What can that be?" they asked each other. As they sat there wondering, the sounds drew closer, until they seemed to come from right outside their house.

"Krunch, grunch. KRUNCH, grunch. KRUNCH, GRUNCH!"

Suddenly a voice boomed out in the grayness.

"Thank you for the favor you did me last night!"

The couple heard the sound of a heavy object being dropped on their doorstep; the crunching noises retreated into the distance.

The husband and wife jumped out of bed and ran to the door. When they opened it they saw a large sack lying there, a sack full of gold coins! They felt the money fall through their fingers, and peered out into the gray morning light. Walking off in the falling snow was the statue of Jizo, without a stitch of clothing on, but for the grass hat he wore on his head.

The Grateful Toad

There was once a wealthy farmer who had three daughters. One morning as he was out inspecting his broad fields, he saw that the water had dried up, and the young rice shoots looked like stalks of hay.

He stared at the ruined rice and sighed miserably.

"I'd give anything," he said to himself, "if I could have water here again. I'd even give one of my daughters." But there was nothing to be done, so he turned and trudged home.

Next morning when he went out to his fields, he saw a stream of clear water gushing into them, and the rice shoots were healthy and green. The farmer remembered what he had said the day before, and looked about him. Suddenly in the lowest fields he caught sight of a huge serpent, gliding through the young green rice.

"What a horror! It must be the monster of the fields!" he thought, and he shook until his stomach was bouncing in terror.

He ran home, where he sat all morning lost in thought, until his eldest daughter brought his lunch.

"Father," she said, "have something to eat."

"I have no stomach for lunch," he said. "The monster of the fields has saved us from drought, but in return I promised him one of you three girls as a wife. Until that is done, I can eat no food."

The girl looked at her father in alarm.

"I'd go anywhere you ask, marry anyone you chose," she cried, "but I cannot marry the monster of the fields." And she ran from the room.

The second daughter appeared in the doorway and gently pressed her father to eat, but he told her he could eat nothing until one of them agreed to marry the monster of the fields. The second daughter fled as her sister had done. The farmer shook with fear and wondered what would become of them all.

The third daughter came into the room, and he told her too that he couldn't eat until either she or one of her sisters agreed to marry the monster of the fields.

"Well, eat then," said the third daughter. "I'd as soon marry the monster of the fields as anyone else."

The father was overjoyed. "What presents shall I buy for your wedding?" he asked.

The daughter replied at once.

"A thousand needles, a plant with a thousand gourds and a thousand strips of wadding."

She bowed, and left her father eating his lunch.

At last the day came for the wedding. The third daughter took the presents and walked down to the lowest rice fields, where the plants were now up to her knees. She attached the thousand cotton strips to the thousand gourds with the thousand pins, and threw them into the water.

"Whoever can sink these thousand gourds," she cried, "is the one I shall marry."

The serpent rose out of the water and swam about trying to sink the gourds, but the sharp pins pierced his skin and he soon bled to death. So no one had to marry him after all.

The girl, however, did not return home after this. Instead she walked away into the mountains. As she climbed the path, she heard a deep croaking.

"Scrooak, scrooak!" it echoed among the trees. "Scrooak, scrooak!"

"It must be the curse of the monster, come to avenge his death," she thought in fear. But there was nothing she could do, and so she walked on.

"Scrooak, scrooak! Scrooak, scrooak!" Suddenly from behind a tree jumped the oldest woman she had ever seen! Her hands were covered with warts, and black eyes bulged from her wide, lined face.

"Young lady! Young lady!" she croaked, bowing low. "I am the wart-toad of the mountain. Time and again my grandchildren were swallowed up by the monster of the rice-fields. You have destroyed him, and the sun may shine or the winds may blow, but now my children and grandchildren, great-grand-children and great-great-grandchildren and all their descendants can live without fear."

The girl smiled and sat down, relieved that it wasn't the monster's curse come to seek revenge. She talked for a while with the old woman, and then rose to go.

"Wait!" the old woman cried. "Young lady, you're too pretty to be traveling alone like this. Take my old woman's skin and you'll be safe from harm."

The girl covered herself with the skin of the wart-toad, and went on to the next village, where she took a job at the mayor's house. From morning till night she swept and cleaned and cooked, wearing the skin of the old woman.

One night the mayor's eldest son noticed a light on in the old woman's room, long after everyone else had gone to sleep. He peeked inside and saw a lovely young woman, reading a book by the lantern-light.

"There are strange things indeed in this world of ours," he thought.

Soon the young man fell ill. The doctors said it was love-sickness and none of them could help him. Finally one doctor suggested that, one by one, all the women in the house take a tray of food to the sick man. "If you marry him to the woman whose tray he eats from," the doctor said, "he'll get well at once."

The mayor had all the serving women of the household take trays of food to his son, but he would not take food from any of them. At last all had taken their turns but the old serving woman.

"She too is a woman after all," said the doctor. "Send her in."

When the girl heard that she was to carry a tray to the young man's room, she took off the toad-woman's skin, bathed and put on fresh clothes and took a tray to the sickroom. As soon as the mayor's son saw her, he sat up and began to eat. They were married, and it is told they lived in peace and happiness for the rest of their lives.

Raw Monkey Liver

Many years ago the daughter of the Lord of the Seas fell ill, and a famous doctor was sent for to cure her. The doctor examined the girl and for a moment looked gravely down at her. Then he turned and walked slowly through the palace halls to the chamber of the Lord of the Seas.

The doctor bowed low before him and stood for a while without speaking. At last he raised his sad eyes and said:

"It is my opinion that this illness is incurable. I know of no medicine, no remedy, no pill, no potion, no lotion or prescription that can save your daughter."

The Lord of the Seas trembled, and the courtiers hid their faces.

"She will most certainly die," he announced solemnly.

"Unless . . . ."

The Lord of the Seas and his courtiers leaned forward eagerly.

"Unless," the doctor continued, "she eats the raw liver of a monkey."

The Lord of the Seas immediately called his most trusted messenger, the turtle, and ordered it to swim to the distant country where the monkeys lived and to bring back a monkey's liver. The turtle swam away, and soon came to an island in the middle of the sea. There it saw a monkey that was building sand castles on the beach.

"Monkey, Mistress Monkey!" cried the turtle. "Have you ever thought of taking a trip to see the world?"

"Why, yes," replied the monkey, "indeed I have."

"But the waters are deep and I cannot swim, so I stay here."

"Why don't you just jump on my back," the turtle said, "and I'll take you to the palace of the Lord of the Seas himself?"

The monkey left her sand castles and her island, and jumped on the turtle's back. Almost before she felt her feet get wet, they were inside the palace gates.

The turtle left the monkey to wait in the garden and hurried away to inform the Lord of the Seas.

The monkey was sniffing red anemones and nibbling leaves of wild sea lettuce, when a blowfish and an octopus swam up to her. In those days they were not at all the way they are now, but looked like any other fishes.

"Thank you, my dear," they bubbled. "It is a fine fine thing you're doing, giving your liver to cure the daughter of the Lord of the Seas. You'll surely be rewarded for it in another life."

"Oh, my goodness, this is dreadful!" the monkey said to the blowfish and the octopus. "But I've left my liver at home, sitting on a coconut high in one of the palm trees at the beach."

The octopus and the blowfish raced to the Lord of the Seas.

"The monkey has left her liver at home," they cried. "It's sitting on a coconut on one of the palm trees at the beach."

The Lord of the Seas' white beard roused the waters. "She'll have to go back and get it." he thundered.

The turtle swam to the monkey, and carried her swiftly back to the island in the middle of the sea. The monkey ran over the sand and climbed to the top of a coconut palm. And there she sat, picking coconuts and drinking their warm milk. Nothing the turtle did would bring her down again.

The turtle was forced to swim home and report what had happened to the Lord of the Seas. The Lord realized that the monkey had tricked them, and he called for the blowfish and the octopus to appear before him. He had the octopus pounded to a pulp, and that is why it has no bones to this day. And the blowfish was beaten until its bones cracked into splinters, and ever since they can be seen sticking out beneath its skin.

But when the daughter of the Lord of the Seas

The Crusty Old Badger

In the outskirts of Shirajima, there was a crusty, crafty old badger, who had been living in the region for several hundred years. Whenever he saw a traveler walking by on the road, the badger would climb up into a tree and turn himself into a wine cask. The traveler would climb up to get it, but when he reached the spot, high up in the branches, the wine cask would have disappeared.

Or if a person drove by in a cart full of fruit or wine, the badger would strew gold coins over the road. The driver would jump down to get the coins, but they would roll away. He would go after them, but the gold would roll on and on, and in the meantime the badger would steal off with the cart and its goods.

But tricks like this were nothing for an old badger who was an expert at disguising himself. There were worse ones he played: for example, the one he played on farmer Sohei, of Ueda village.

Sohei was a kind man and a hard worker, proud of his sharp wits and his beautiful thick hair. One day in winter, he decided to visit the priest who lived on the mountain. He rose before daylight, dressed, combed his thick black hair and tied it in a knot at the back of his head. Quietly, so as not to wake the rest of the family, he stole out of the door and walked into the cold.

As he was climbing up the mountain path, he suddenly heard a voice behind him.

"Sohei-san! Sohei-san! Where are you going so early in the morning?"

Startled, Sohei looked around. He saw a plump young woman, carrying a package wrapped in cloth. She ran out from behind the trees and caught up with him.

"I thought I'd make a visit to the priest," Sohei answered. He looked closely at the woman and scratched his head.

"Excuse me for my rudeness," he added, "but I'm afraid I haven't the slightest idea who you are."

"Oh, my goodness! And yet I know you so well!"
The woman's fat cheeks turned pink with embarrass-
ment. "Oh, well, that's the way it is, I suppose. It
doesn't really matter, though, does it?"

Before Sohei could reply, she continued:

"I do hate to ask you a favor when you're on your
way to the priest's, but could you just hold this package for a moment? I must go up the hill a ways, but
I'll be right back. It's very important."

Without waiting for an answer, she carefully
handed him her package, and ran off up the hill.

Sohei stood and waited, guarding the precious
package. Day dawned, and the sky grew light. Then
clouds appeared and flakes of snow began to fall.
Still Sohei waited.

Meanwhile, his family had begun to worry that he
hadn't returned home, and several of them set out
to look for him. What was their surprise to find him
standing peacefully under a tree by the path, holding a package.

"Whatever are you doing here?" they cried.
"We've been waiting and waiting."

Sohei told them about the young woman. "The
package seemed very important to her," he said.
"Let's wait just a bit longer."

But Sohei's family had no intention of staying out in the cold.

"Why don't we open it and see what's inside?" someone suggested.

Sohei did not want to open a package that did not belong to him, but it was taken from him. The cloth was untied and everyone looked inside.

They found nothing but a stone!

Sohei stared. At first he was surprised, then he became angry, and his anger grew until he was purple with fury.

"This is the work of that old badger!" he cried out. "From now on, it's going to have to watch out for me!"

After this, Sohei spent his spare time combing Shirajima for the old badger. His family tried again and again to dissuade him. "You'll only be sorry for it later," they said. "Remember how the badger bewitched Seicho, and left him standing naked on top of his roof? Remember how Heihachi tried to catch the badger, but was caught in his own trap and left tangled up in it for two days?"

But Sohei refused to listen to their warnings and kept looking.

At last, one noonday at the beginning of spring,

his efforts seemed about to be rewarded. He had dressed in his best clothes, had had his thick hair carefully oiled and combed, and set off to do some shopping in the castle town. As he was passing through the gates of the town, he came upon a beggar, sitting by the moat with his begging bowl. As Sohei went by, the man suddenly began to beg at the top of his voice. Tears ran down his cheeks as he clutched Sohei's jacket and raised his bowl.

Sohei stopped and looked at the beggar. There was something strange about him. Sohei stared at his round glittering eyes. Suddenly Sohei jumped back. He was sure this was the badger in another disguise!

Sohei remembered the long hours he had stood in the cold holding the badger's package, and the blood rushed to his head in anger. He raised his walking stick and began to beat the beggar.

But if the beggar was, indeed, the badger in disguise, he was very slow in changing back to his true shape and running away. Instead, he only cried out with a pitiful voice, as he tried to fend off the blows of Sohei's stick.

"Please, sir!" he cried, and his voice was as thin and dry as autumn grasses, "I'm not a badger at all! I'm only a poor beggar who has had nothing to eat for two days. I had no strength to go on, and I came to rest here at the edge of the town, only to be beaten by a stranger whom I've never seen or harmed."

The beggar's voice weakened and died. He fell back on the ground.

Sohei stood and looked at what he had done, and the blood slowly drained from his face.

"Aieeeeeeee!" he cried. He bent over the beggar's still body and sobbed as though his heart would break.

Just then, a priest passed by. Seeing Sohei's distress, he gently asked what was the matter. Sohei raised his tear-stained face to the priest and told him what had happened.

The priest was thoughtful for a few moments. Then he looked at Sohei and said quietly:

"Your tears cannot bring this man back to life; but the strength of prayers can help save his soul. You should become a monk and rid yourself of your sins by praying for him."

Sohei hung his head. There was nothing he could do but agree. The priest shaved Sohei's head, took his clothes and gave him a monk's robe in return. Then he placed a pair of wooden clappers in his hands.

"Day and night for the rest of your life," the priest told Sohei, "you must recite these words of prayer.

Namu Amida Butsu
Namu Amida Butsu

In this way, the poor beggar's soul will have some hope of being saved."

With these words, the priest turned and left. Sohei sat by the moat and recited the prayer, and the hours passed as if in a dream.

Suddenly, he thought he heard someone calling his name. Sohei looked up. He was surrounded by a whole crowd of villagers, pointing at him and giggling behind their hands.

Sohei looked down. There was no beggar beside him at all, but only a small statue of Jizo, which he was holding in his arms. No monk's robes covered him, but only a few strips of dirty rags hid his nakedness. He had been tricked again by the crafty old badger!

Sohei rubbed his head, then looked in shock at the circle of laughing villagers. His beautiful hair was gone! The badger had shaved his head as bald and smooth as a stone in the river.

45

The Cloth of
a Thousand
Feathers

There was once a woodcutter named Karoku, who
lived with his old mother high up in the mountains.
One day when winter was drawing near, Karoku set
off for town to buy a quilt. He came down the mountain, through the village, passed the first rice fields,
and when he reached the edge of the valley, he saw
something white fluttering by the roadside.

Karoku drew near and found that it was a crane,
caught fast in a snare, and struggling under the
strings which held it down. He took pity on the bird

and carefully loosened the strings to set it free. Just as the bird was almost out, the owner of the snare appeared.

"What are you doing, meddling with other people's property?" the man shouted. "That crane belongs to me!"

"I felt sorry for it," said Karoku, "and only wanted to help it. Look," he went on, "I was going to buy a quilt with this money. Will you take it for the crane instead?"

And so the crane was sold to Karoku. As soon as it was safely in his hands, Karoku set the bird free, and watched it fly back to the mountains.

There was nothing left for him to do but to go home, with not even a string from the snare to show for his money. The first bitter winds of the year blew coldly through him, and Karoku thought of the long winter nights to come.

The moment he walked into the house his mother asked him about the quilt, and Karoku was forced to tell her how he had spent the money.

"That was a kind thing you did," his mother said, smiling. "I'm proud to have you as my son."

But his kindness brought them no warmth, and they were cold that night as they lay in their beds.

The next day toward evening, a lovely young woman came to their door. Her skin was as white as the finest rice, her soft eyes were black as blackest coal. Her neck was long and slender.

"Kind people," she said, "it is late and I have no place to stay. May I spend the night at your house?"

Karoku stared at her in amazement.

"Our miserable house is not fit for such a beautiful woman to sleep in!" he cried, and he pointed out to her the road to the mansion of the rich lord who lived in the valley.

"But, sir," pleaded the woman, "I am tired and want only to rest. May I not stay here?"

Karoku and his mother let her come in, and she slept peacefully through the night, wrapped in her traveling clothes. Next morning at breakfast the woman asked if she might have a word with Karoku.

When he agreed, she said quietly:

"Would it please you if we were to become husband and wife?"

"Husband and wife!" Karoku exclaimed. "In all my life I've never even seen anyone as lovely as you. And here you are asking to be my wife! Do you know what my life is like?" He continued, "Each morning I ask myself how we will get enough to eat, and in the evening I wonder how we will manage to get through the next day. How can you want to live such a life?"

"I want only to be your wife," the woman said, and her voice was as soft as the cooing of a bird.

"But it's impossible!" said Karoku.

His mother, who had been listening, now spoke.

"If you want it so much," she said to the woman, "you are welcome to marry my son. But we are poor, and the life will be hard for you."

So it happened that Karoku and the woman were married.

As winter wore on, the weather became worse and worse, and before long all three shivered with cold in their beds. One day the young woman said to her husband:

"Shut me in the back room for three days, and do not look inside during that time."

The mother and son thought this very odd but nevertheless did as the wife asked. On the evening of the third day she opened the door and came out. Her face was pale and wan, and her kimono hung loosely about her thin body. In her hands she held a beautiful cloth made all of feathers, which she held out to them.

"This is a cloth of a thousand feathers," she said to her husband. "Take it to the lord down in the valley, and sell it to him for two thousand pieces of gold."

Karoku could only stare at his wife. Without a word, he took the cloth and carried it to the lord's mansion.

The lord was annoyed that a lowly woodcutter had come to see him.

"Get on with your business," he snapped.

Karoku slowly unwrapped the cloth of a thousand feathers and spread it out.

The lord's eyes bulged from their sockets. Never had he seen such exquisite work.

"You may have it for two thousand pieces of gold," Karoku mumbled.

"It is easily worth three," the lord said. "I'll give you the two thousand at once."

Karoku swallowed hard and nodded. Two thousand gold pieces! It was more than he had ever dreamed of, more than he could count!

"And I'd like another," the lord added.

Karoku gasped, but there was nothing he could do. "I'll have to ask my wife," he stuttered.

"It matters not whom you ask," the lord said. "I

expect another one." When Karoku left the house, his heart was heavy despite the riches in his pocket, for he had seen how making the cloth had weakened his wife.

That night, at supper, Karoku told her that the lord had demanded another cloth. Her black eyes filled with tears, but she nodded her head.

"This time," she said, "you must lock me in the back room for a week. And on no account open the door before I come out."

Karoku looked down at her bowed head and slender neck, and told himself that he would never ask her for another thing and would always treat her with care and kindness.

The next day his wife went into the back room, and Karoku and his mother locked the door behind her. Four days went by, then five, then six. On the afternoon of the seventh day, Karoku could stand it no longer. He listened at the door, but there was no sound. He called out to his wife, but there was no answer. At last, he unlocked the door and rushed inside.

There stood his wife, not a woman at all, but a naked crane, whose every feather had been plucked out. The bird had plucked her own feathers and knotted them together to make the cloths. She had just finished the second one when Karoku entered the room.

Sadly, the bird turned her long plucked neck and looked at her human husband.

"Here is the cloth you promised the lord," she said. "I am the crane you rescued many months ago. In gratitude I came to be your wife and live with you until we both grew old. But now that you have seen me in my true form, I must return to my own land."

As she spoke, there was the sound of flapping wings outside the window, and a thousand cranes descended from the sky. The featherless bird was lifted onto the spread wings of a crane, and they all flew away toward the setting sun.

The Old Woman
in the Cottage

Many years ago, there lived a young man named
Juhei.

One cold winter day he decided to leave his village
and go shopping in the town a few miles away. He
woke up very early, when the sky was barely light,
and quietly left the house.

Juhei trudged over the snowy path, up toward the
cliff at the top of the mountain. All at once he heard
a noise some distance ahead. It was still too dark to
see much more than black shapes; Juhei lay down on
his stomach and crawled cautiously forward. On the
path not twenty feet ahead crouched a still black

form. It was a fox, busily gnawing on something. A dead mouse? A potato? Juhei couldn't see.

"I'll bet that's the fox that's been stealing food from the village these past few weeks," he thought. "I'll give it a scare it won't forget."

He looked about. On the snow nearby was a good-sized rock. Juhei picked it up, took aim and threw. The rock flew toward its mark; it nicked the fox's nose and landed smack on its food. The fox was so astonished it leaped into the air, turned tail and raced away toward the cliff edge where it jumped off! Down, down it fell, until finally it landed with a splash in the icy pool below.

Juhei laughed from the cliff top as he watched the fox thrash about in the water. It reached the rocks by the shore and climbed up, dripping. Hardly stopping to shake itself, the fox scurried into the woods and disappeared.

Juhei gaily continued on his way to town. He finished his shopping early, and started for home, thinking he could get there well before dark.

"Ah," he said to himself, "if I'm home in time for supper, I can tell them about what I did to the fox this morning. That's one beast that won't be bothering us for a while."

Juhei had walked about a mile, when the sky suddenly began to darken; another mile and he could hardly see the trees. He began to make his way up the mountain, but it became so dark that he couldn't even see his feet beneath him.

Juhei stopped and looked about. Some distance away, he could barely make out a yellow light that glimmered palely in the darkness.

"Well," he muttered, "I'll try to borrow a torch or a lamp, and if that doesn't work, I'll just have to spend the night there. I hope at least it's warm inside."

He headed for the light and after a few minutes came to a small cottage. He peeked in at the window. An old woman, at least eighty years old, sat inside by the fire, carefully painting her teeth with black lacquer. Her hair was as white as the new-fallen snow, but her teeth were like those of a young woman. Not one seemed to be missing.

Juhei walked around to the door and knocked.

"Excuse me!" he called. "Is anyone here?"

After quite a while, he heard the woman get up from her chair. She walked to the door, opened it and stood looking at him.

"I beg your pardon," he said. "My name is Juhei

and I'm from the village just over the mountain. I'm on my way home from town, but it's gotten too dark to see. Do you have a torch or a lantern I could borrow? I'll bring it back tomorrow."

The old woman did not reply but stared calmly at Juhei, who stood before her shivering with cold.

"Maybe she's deaf," he thought. He repeated what he had said, a bit louder this time, but the woman still looked at him, remaining silent. It was some moments before she finally spoke:

"I have neither a torch nor a lamp," she said.

Juhei shivered.

"May I perhaps spend the night here, then?" he stuttered.

The old woman replied, slowly choosing her words.

"I don't have a blanket for you, so you can't stay the night. But you can sit before the fire for a while."

Juhei entered the cottage and sat himself by the fire, facing the old woman. Ignoring her guest, she calmly opened wide her mouth and went back to painting her teeth with black lacquer. Juhei watched her in the firelight and felt uneasy.

The fire began to die down. Juhei wondered what he would do when it went out. The old woman continued to blacken her teeth. Juhei couldn't help watching.

Suddenly, the old woman stretched her neck forward and her face came toward him; her black eyes grew as round as round.

"Yaaaaaaaaahh!" she yelped, and her beautiful black-lacquered teeth sank into Juhei's nose.

"Aiieeeeee!" Juhei jumped up in pain, stumbled against something and fell down.

But what was going on here? Juhei was splashing about in the middle of the very same icy pond the fox had fallen into that morning. The old woman was the fox in disguise. She had simply tricked him!

Juhei swam over to the rocks by the shore. Shaking and shivering he pulled himself out of the water.

He was blue with cold. Only his nose was red, swollen and painful. Juhei looked about him. The sky was dark, and the cold path home lay before him in the snowy shadows of the trees.

The
Two Statues
of Kannon

There was once a mountain witch who lived high in
the cryptomeria forests above the village of Yasunaga. Travelers passing in the vicinity would hear the
sound of a child crying from behind the trees, but
when they followed the sound, out popped the witch
and ate them up. Before long, people stopped going
to Yasunaga, and the villagers were cut off from the
world.

In the village there lived a man by the name of

Uheita. One day he walked into the forest, and he, too, heard the sound of a child crying, but when he went to see, the crying stopped and out came the mountain witch.

Uheita looked down at the witch.

"Good day, grandmother," he said. "What is a lone woman like yourself doing out here in the wild woods?"

The witch looked up at the big man.

"Oh," she said in a sweet squeaking voice, "I've wandered off the path and lost my way. I don't know what to do."

"Why, a little person like you will be easy enough to carry," laughed Uheita, and before she could say no, he lifted her on his back, pinned her legs tight against him and, holding fast to her arms, set off carrying her piggyback.

"Fine," squeaked the witch, for there was nothing she could do, "but you must let me down when I ask you to."

"I'll let you down, of course," he replied, smiling.

Along the path they lumbered, until they came to the outskirts of the village. The witch was hungry.

"Let me down here," she ordered, and thought

with pleasure of how delicious Uheita would taste.

But he only held her tighter. "Not yet," he answered. "The village is still far away."

"Let me down, let me down! My back is sore; my arms hurt."

"Hang on; it'll soon be over."

"Now, now. It hurts!"

"We're almost there!"

And so they came to Uheita's house. With the witch still held fast to his back with one hand, Uheita quickly shuttered the windows and locked the doors. He lit a fire in the fireplace, and when the flames were roaring, let go of the witch and threw her in.

Crickle, crackle she burned. "Ai chichichichichichi-aaah!" she screeched. Then she jumped right out and screamed at Uheita, baring her large, sharp yellow teeth:

"I am the Witch of the Mountains! No mere human can fool with me!" She jumped over the table, twirled past the chairs, swung from the rafters, kicked at the windows, banged on the pots, turned a somersault and disappeared.

"Now where could she have gone?" Uheita wondered, and he began to search the house. High and low he looked, until at last he came to the family shrine. Where there had always been a single statue of the goddess Kannon before, now there were two, exactly alike.

He looked and looked at the statues, but he could find no difference between them.

"Which one is the real one; which one is the witch?"

He stared for a long time at the two statues; then he jumped up.

"Of course!" he cried. "All I have to do is offer them rice with red beans in it. The real Kannon always smiles and reaches out her right hand for it. I'll cook up some rice at once."

When the rice was ready, Uheita put it into a bowl and set it before the two Kannons. The golden lips of one of the statues slowly curved into a smile, and her right hand reached out for the food.

"Aha!" cried Uheita. He grabbed the false statue and ran with it to the stove, where he dumped it into a pot of boiling water.

The beautiful Kannon suddenly turned into the mountain witch, who screamed until the house shook. But Uheita only covered her up with the lid and held it down tightly with both hands. After a while the witch stopped struggling, and Uheita looked into the pot.

The water and the witch had both disappeared, and nothing remained but a small puddle of black tar.

The Mirror

There was once a young man who loved his father very much. Soon after the young man married, his father died, and the son was filled with sorrow.

Several months passed, and one day the son had to go to the capital on business. Strolling about the city, he happened to walk by a store that sold mirrors. The young man had never seen a mirror before, and glanced at the strange objects as he passed by. To his astonishment he saw his own dead father, whom he resembled greatly, staring out at him from the frame as though he were still alive!

"Father!" cried the young man. "What are you doing here in the capital?"

There was no reply, but the young man went into the store, bought the mirror at once and carried it carefully back to his village. Once home, he set it

inside the family shrine and prayed to it every morning with great devotion.

His wife noticed how frequently he prayed at the
shrine, and one morning after her husband had gone
out, she looked inside. The face of a lovely young
woman met her eyes!

When her husband returned home, she was in a
fury.

"You've brought back the image of another
woman from the capital, and keep her enshrined in
a gilded frame!" she cried. "How can you do such a
thing?"

"A woman?" the young man asked in surprise.
"That's my own dead father!" He went to the shrine
and looked into the glass to make sure. With relief
he saw his father's face looking out at him. His wife
took the mirror.

"Your father!" she cried. "That's a woman!"

They argued back and forth, and there was no
solution. At last they decided to take the mirror to
the wise nun who lived in the temple at the edge of
the village. The husband told the nun his story and
the wife told hers. The nun asked to see the mirror.
She took it in her hands and looked into the glass.

"Why," she said, "the woman has repented and

become a nun. It's best that she remain here in the temple where she belongs."

With that, the nun put the mirror safely in a box and closed the lid.

Picking Mountain Pears

There was once a mother who lived with her three sons. One summer she fell sick, and as time went by she grew weaker and weaker. Her sons were most unhappy.

One day the mother called them to her. "I know that I would get well at once," she told her sons, "if only I could taste a mountain pear."

The oldest son jumped up. "I'll go," he said, and he set off toward the mountains. He walked and walked until he came to a boulder at the edge of a great forest, and on top of the boulder sat an old old woman.

"Where are you going, young man?" she croaked.

"I'm going to pick mountain pears for my sick mother," the eldest son replied.

"Then listen to what I tell you," said the old old woman. "You will come to a place where the path forks in three, and beside each fork there is a clump of bamboo. One clump will rustle its leaves saying, 'No, no gasa gasa.' Do not follow this path. Another clump will rustle the words, 'Go not gasa gasa.' Do not follow this path either. But the leaves of one of them will rustle: 'Go on, gasa gasa.' That will be the path you should follow."

The boy thanked her and walked on his way. He came to the place where the road forked in three, but he paid no attention to the old woman's instructions and so chose the wrong path.

He saw a crow building its nest in a bare withered pine. The crow looked down at the eldest son. "No, no gasa gasa," it called.

"That's a strange way of cawing," thought the boy, and walked on.

He came to a vine heavy with yellow gourds. "Go not gasa gasa," rattled the gourds.

"That's a strange way of rattling," thought the eldest son, and walked on.

He walked past a maple tree covered with red leaves, over a stream and around a bend, and there, beside a green green pond, stood a huge pear tree laden with mountain pears.

The eldest son climbed up the tree and reached out to pick some pears, but his shadow fell on the water below and woke the monster of the pond from his sleep. The monster raised its head out of the water, opened wide its jaws and gobbled up the eldest son.

The mother and her two sons waited at home, but the eldest son did not return, so the second son set out. He met the old old woman sitting on the boulder, but he too ignored her advice, just as his brother had done. He came to the fork in the road and followed the other wrong path. He walked by a crow building its nest in a withered pine. "No, no gasa gasa," it called, but he walked on. He came to a vine heavy with yellow gourds. "Go not gasa gasa," they rattled, but he walked on. He walked past a maple tree covered with red leaves, over the stream, around the bend, climbed the pear tree and was gobbled up just like his brother.

The mother and the youngest son waited and waited, but the brothers did not return, so the youngest son stood up and said that he would go.

The mother took his hand and in a voice hardly stronger than a whisper she said: "You mustn't go, you're all I have left."

But the boy knew that his mother could only be cured by eating a mountain pear, so when he saw that she had fallen asleep, he stole out of the door.

He met the old old woman who sat on the boulder.

"Have you seen my brothers?" he asked. "They set off to pick mountain pears for our mother, who is sick."

"If they haven't returned," the old old woman said, "it's because they did not listen to my words. Now listen carefully and do as I say."

The youngest son heard her advice and walked on until he came to the triple fork in the path.

"No, no gasa gasa," rustled the bamboo beside one path.

"Go not gasa gasa," rustled the leaves of the plant beside another path.

"Go on, gasa gasa," rustled the leaves of the bamboo by the third path, and the youngest son took this path.

He came to a crow building its nest in a pine. "Go on!" it called.

He came to a vine heavy with yellow gourds. "Go on!" rattled the gourds.

The youngest son walked past a maple tree covered with red leaves, and he noticed a straw doll lying on the ground beside it. He picked up the doll, hung it on his belt and walked on.

As he was crossing a stream, a piece of a broken bowl came tumbling down in the water, and floated nearby. The youngest son picked it up and put it in his pocket. He rounded a bend and there, beside a green green pond, was the huge pear tree laden with mountain pears. A breeze blew through the leaves of the tree, and with each gust he heard these words:

> *Don't climb the east side,*
> *Danger on the west side,*
> *Shadow on the north side,*
> *Climb up the south side.*

So the youngest son climbed up the south side of the tree and picked some delicious mountain pears, which he dropped to the grass below. When he felt he had picked enough, he began to climb down, but he accidentally moved over to the north side of the tree, where his shadow fell on the water.

The pond monster woke up, raised its head from the green water and opened its jaws to swallow the youngest son. But the boy grabbed fast to the branch and hoisted himself up, so all the monster could gobble was the straw doll which hung from the youngest son's belt.

The monster dropped back into the pond, then rose again, and its head reached toward the boy. Then suddenly it turned, thrashing and flailing its tail so that the green pond turned white with foam. The straw doll had stuck in its throat; the monster was choking!

Its neck shook and twisted; it gasped for breath. All at once it spewed the straw doll onto the shore. Right behind it came the second brother, and the eldest brother after him. The monster shuddered and sank beneath the water and did not come up again.

The two brothers lay on the shore by the pond, their faces as blue as the sky, their bodies cold and still. The youngest son took the broken bowl and scooped up some water, which he put to his brothers' blue lips. At once they awoke and became as alive and well as before.

Together the three brothers walked back down the

mountain, carrying the mountain pears among them. Their mother awoke as they came in the door, and no sooner did she take one bite of a mountain pear than she became completely well again.

The Strange
Folding Screen

In Kami there once lived a man named Kikusaburo, who inherited vast rice fields and mountain forests from his parents. Kikusaburo was not a bad sort, but he hated work and he loved pleasure. As the years went by, he was forced to sell his fields and forests to pay for his debts, and finally he had nothing left but his manor house and one mountain.

And yet he continued in the same way of life and his debts kept piling up. Kikusaburo was finally forced to sell the remaining mountain. He rose early one morning and went off to survey the land, so that he would know exactly how much land and how much forest there was and set a proper price on it.

He climbed all morning, measuring the land where he had played as a small boy. About midday, he came to a small river, lined with beautiful trees with foliage so thick that even the noonday sun was blocked out and the river banks lay in cool deep shade.

Near the foot of the mountain, the river flowed into a lake, where Kikusaburo watched great numbers of frogs splashing about. The frogs had lived there longer than he could remember; every year at the beginning of summer, their sorrowful voices filled the air, so that the people had named this water the Lake of the Croaking Frogs.

Kikusaburo was tired from his morning of measuring the land and counting trees. As he sat by the lake in the shadow of large rocks and watched the frogs, his eyelids grew heavy and he lay his head on his arms and slept.

Suddenly, he felt a cold hand on his shoulder. Kikusaburo looked up. An old man with a face like one of the river frogs stood before him. His green kimono was draped around him like water weeds, and water ran in streams from the hem.

"Kikusaburo, sir," he said, bowing, "I am the chief of the frogs in this lake. I'm dreadfully sorry to interrupt your nap, but I have come on behalf of my brothers to ask a great favor of you. We saw you counting trees this morning, and measuring the land, and it would seem that you want to sell the mountain. We beg you not to let it go. Whoever buys it will cut down the trees, and the hot sun will bake the river valley dry. The rains will turn the bare mountain slopes to mud, and the mud will flow into the clear water of our lake. We will not be able to survive."

"Why, he's right," thought Kikusaburo. He looked about him at the cool green trees and the peaceful lake. "I'm not surprised the frogs like to live here," he mused.

The old frog stood before him, his wrinkled face filled with sorrow.

"I beg you, Kikusaburo, sir," he pleaded. Bowing low, he grasped Kikusaburo by the hand.

Brrrrrrrr! The frog's hand was so icy cold that it sent a chill through Kikusaburo, and he came to himself with a start.

He looked around. There was no sign of the old man. Only the peaceful tree-lined lake lay before him, and here and there a frog croaked in the shadows.

"It must have been a dream!" he thought.

But if it had been a dream, it had seemed very real, and Kikusaburo walked home with a strange, heavy sadness in his heart.

The next day, Kikusaburo decided not to sell his land. Instead he went to an antique dealer and sold the ancient vases, lamps, teacups and scrolls that were in his house. Piece by piece he sold them off, until all of his debts were paid.

Now the house was completely bare. Nothing remained but a screen of blank white paper, which wasn't worth selling, or even looking at. Kikusaburo wandered alone through the empty rooms. He picked up the screen and stood it at the head of his bed, then crawled under the covers and fell fast asleep.

It was just before daylight. Kikusaburo heard strange noises; it sounded as if he were surrounded by a whole horde of chirping, croaking, bellowing frogs! He opened his eyes and sat up.

The dawn light had begun to filter softly into the bare room. Kikusaburo shook his head, yawned, and got out of bed.

What was this? The floor was covered with wet footprints, especially around the screen. The screen! It was no longer blank, but was covered with pictures of frogs. Sitting, swimming, leaping or sleeping, they seemed so real that he could almost hear their voices. When Kikusaburo looked closer he saw that the ink was still wet, as though the pictures had just been painted.

Kikusaburo sat and stared at the screen. After a while, he left it and went to putter about the house, nailing in the boards where they stuck out, cleaning the rubbish from the garden, polishing the door knobs. But he was constantly drawn back to the screen. He would sit and look at the frogs, then burst out laughing, shake his head and go back to his chores.

Word of the frog screen soon spread throughout the village, and many people came to see it.

Eventually art experts from the city found their way out to the house. They sighed deeply as they looked at the screen, and remarked on the skill and beauty of the brushstrokes. As time went on, Kiku-saburo was more than once offered fortunes for the screen. And yet for some reason, he couldn't bring himself to sell it, and kept it with him by his bed. He began to work every day. He rose early to clear the vegetable patch of weeds or to see to the spring rice planting, and only stopped working late at night, when he fell exhausted into bed.

The years passed, and Kikusaburo regained the fortune he had lost. He married and had children, who worked with him on the land, and cared for him when he got old.

Kikusaburo died one morning in early summer. His family noticed that the screen seemed to have faded since the night before. Hour by hour the ink became fainter, until soon there was nothing left but a screen of blank white paper.

Many years have passed, and the screen has disappeared, but the Lake of the Croaking Frogs is still clear and deep, and early each summer the air is filled with the sound of croaking frogs.

Bang, Garrett, comp.

C11160

Men from the village deep in the mountains and other
Japanese folk tales, translated and illustrated by Garrett
Bang. New York, Macmillan [1973]

84 p. illus. 23 cm. $4.95

CONTENTS: Men from the village deep in the mountains. —
Patches. — The stone statue and the grass hat. — The grateful
toad. — Raw monkey liver. — The crusty old badger. — The cloth of a
thousand feathers. — The old woman in the cottage. — The two statues
of Kannon. — The mirror. — Picking mountain pears. — The strange
folding screen.

1. Tales, Japanese. [2. Folklore—Japan]   I. Title.